Judge Jones Resurgam

By
Meryl M Williams

ISBN: 9781917601092

THE AUTHOR - MERYL M WILLIAMS b1966

Meryl was initially a trained and qualified cell biologist, working in medical research at three separate Universities in the UK and overseas. She has utilised many of her skills, plus her lived experience of mental health, to bring this sequel to The Judge Jones Trilogy to the public eye. This book is specialised, based firmly on non fiction with fictitious characters but Meryl feels it needed doing.

Meryl has given a number of poetry and music events to friends to raise money for charities plus she has written for local newsletters. Meryl lives quietly in Bath, Somerset.

Other works by this Poet and Author

Novellas

The Judge Jones Trilogy
My Lady's Sovereign
Mortymer House

Poetry and Photographs

Moods in Bloom
Treasure Within - A Memoir
A Waterfall of Words

ACKNOWLEDGMENTS

A huge thank you must go out from the depths of my heart to all psychiatric nurses, doctors, nursing assistants, pharmacists and lawyers who made this journey possible. For information with respect to the Mental Health Act (1983) I am indebted to both my support staff in the community plus the British NHS website. For insider information on the harsh realities of life with this issue I would like to thank the testimonies of all service users I have met.

JUDGE JONES RESURGAM

CONTENTS

JUDGE JONES RESURGAM

I. Whatever it takes

Episode 1 - A long haul flight

Judge Jones and his new wife Caroline sat down to dinner that evening while enjoying an agreeable discussion.

"Basically", argued Jones digesting his meal, "whatever Marj may or may not have done to me, we are divorced and that won't change. There were statistics for knife crime in England and the figures are appalling. It may be a coincidence but it's a risk we all face."

"Let's contact Michael Charles", suggested Caroline, "it's springtime in England and it will be time to wet their baby's head. Perhaps he knows more, it's surprising he didn't call".

Michael, the fine City barrister, was firm but fair.

"Your Honour", he began with his wig beside him on his desk, "you're onto an exciting new life. Jones please don't wish yourself back. Marj has served a full sentence, she is now discharged and living near the family you appear to have forgotten. If you return now it could put her in jeopardy, we can't afford to have her re-offend or put your life at risk again. Yes another lawyer has been stabbed but the Law people would never let you judge a case concerning your own former marriage. It's not appropriate that you attempt it although I have no power to prevent your return.

Pemberton is very capable and we have far more serious cases to deal with".

Michael spoke decisively as he was defending a whole series of offences in connection with Kylie Smythe. Even though the young lady was serving a sentence for possessing and supplying weapons, she still had contacts with friends outside the prison and arrests were still being made that linked in with her crime. Michael did not intend to confide any of this to Jones, these new cases were sensitive and confidential and Jones had left his field to pursue a life of ease on a generous pension. Michael had often felt that Jones had been overly severe and domineering, the newly married barrister enjoyed standing up to his former colleague for the first time and Michael found a new strength of will as he paused to think about his wife Holly and their newborn son.

Jones switched off the computer and sat back in one of Caroline's deck chairs. In Australia where they lived, the sun was just setting at the same time as Michael had been starting his day back home in City Court House. Jones was flabbergasted by this new assertiveness on the part of Michael, then the former judge was suddenly homesick and grumbled to himself that Michael was below the belt in suggesting that he, Jones should have forgotten his own grandson.

"Well I admit I wasn't expecting so much resistance from Michael", said a startled Caroline, "but is there an alternative?" Jones gazed out to sea and hurt so bad he tried to visualise England across the water. He reached for his lukewarm mug of coffee then spoke again.

"I can see a careers coach but I was once offered the chance to teach law back at Oxbridge. Then there's law reform but it might seem very dry to a young, exciting woman like yourself. Marj was a bit too accepting, what I love about you Caz is that you question things, you're no doormat".

Caroline was deeply touched then asked would he have to do any extra training? They continued to discuss their future, then he spoke with nostalgia about his earlier years before his first marriage, when he was training for the bar.

"But Caz", he queried, "how do you feel about the British climate? Will your great nephew manage the farm and will you miss your beach barbecues?"

Episode 2 - New every morning

The next morning Caroline and Cedric Jones awoke to a beautiful sunrise at the back of their villa as the former Judge realised what new hope came with a new day.

"No Caroline you're right", he said "there's no going back but I feel that I must do something. I am unfamiliar with Australian law, although I recognise the importance of citizenship so what can I do if I also know nothing about farming?" Caroline always encouraged her new husband to enjoy cooking now that he had time to indulge but she said to him that Miles, her great-nephew, was born and raised on the farm so it would be in good hands. Cedric fixed a healthy breakfast of grilled tomatoes with avocado on wholegrain, sourdough toast then sat down with his laptop to weigh up the pros and cons of relocating back to England for what seemed like a desirable yet uncertain future.

He discovered that the luxury and ease of his new life was beginning to pall but also realised that he just needed the positive stress of an activity without the pressures of a High Court career. He had to reinvent himself while accepting that he was getting on in life and the thought of the journey back to England was too daunting at this stage. Then he checked out the cost of flights and insurance which really did deter him from this retrograde step. No, it was the shock of that International news about stabbings in England that roused his old passion for law work, leaving him to think that his interest was starting to border on the macabre.

His first task then was to write down his interests, some from a long time ago, to focus his mind into discovering what he really enjoyed when outside of City Court House. With his new wife he had the perfect, luxury villa a short step from a beautiful, private beach with guaranteed sunshine so just as he was typing this up Caroline came into his study to ask if he would like to have a dog to walk? Yes, that would give him a hobby and a focus while giving him exercise as he mustn't gain excessive weight. The other hobby he found by scanning a long list was horse riding - perfect for spring or autumn evenings along the beach and he knew that Miles kept stables with mounts for hire.

All in all he felt he'd had a productive morning, putting himself to rights then at the end of the day after a long walk taking in the sea air he finally picked up the neglected Sydney Morning Herald, Caroline's daily newspaper. Caroline took a call from her great-nephew Miles so took the opportunity to book pony trekking for herself and Cedric for the weekend. Miles said that once they'd built up their confidence, there was a group available that went on weekends near the shoreline as well as inland to local beauty spots away from the city. Meanwhile, Cedric reviewed the what's on pages of the newspaper and went online to book tickets for Sydney Opera House.

"Caroline, they're doing Handel's Messiah for Advent then some Verdi in the New Year. I booked the seats in the gods as it's meant to be the best for sound as well as economy."

Caroline had another look at the what's on pages and suggested some art classes that were starting for the autumn term in a nearby church hall. She explained that she had put on an exhibition once with help from Miles' mother with art inspired by the farm and stables, using the facility at St Catherine's.

"I can't draw for toffee", she smiled, "but I loved the freer watercolour we did where it was suggested, rather than perfectly stated. There are some of my old paintings in the loft and one picture showing the ponies on the beach, in the guest bedroom."

Episode 3 - Pleasures Persist

It was that time of year for Cedric to have his annual review with a family doctor. He discovered that he needed no further medication, all his results were fine and his health care team considered that he was adapting to the new climate, with his new lifestyle, in a creditable way. Jones was a little uneasy with his life of luxury and ease. Caroline found him fussing over the cost of air conditioning which she reassured him they could well afford. Caz herself misapprehended the amount of Jones income as his pension was not as generous as his former salary. He often kept quiet as he didn't like to argue about money but when the bills arrived at each month's end there was little left for extravagance. Jones really had to gear himself up to grumble that they were being overcharged for the Pony Trekking then he cut it back to once a month.

In addition, Jones was still paying off their luxury cruise to England with the added expense of their onboard wedding. Finally he explained to his new wife that economies were needed but her response was to assert that at least it kept him occupied, away from under her feet, and it was good for him to have a hobby.

Caroline was in the happy position of receiving a comfortable income from the farm she'd inherited, with her great-nephew working the land but she was squeamish about money after an impoverished childhood when the farm was not as prosperous. Then more happy news came in the form of a rise to Cedric's pension from England as it was index linked, so cheerfully the couple went to the Opera House.

Two weeks later, Cedric had completed the first term of his watercolour painting class and his tutor began to prepare the group for an exhibition at Christmas. There was to be an opening ceremony with festive treats then a week of portraiture followed by a week of landscapes for the general public. Cedric had painted seascapes with dramatic sunsets or other light effects and the tutor was encouraging him to put prices on his work as there would be visitors wanting to buy something new and original. This was a time when Jones was really enjoying himself, he loved organising his work, giving each piece a title, getting all the paintings framed and deciding on their value. Then the tutor encouraged Cedric to photograph his paintings to add them to the catalogue that was being produced with all the exhibits from the whole class. The tutor said that if paintings were hard to sell, the catalogue might be sold instead as those art lovers on smaller incomes would appreciate this collection all together in the one paperback book. The whole was collated and Jones was really delighted with the results.

As Jones prepared for his first Christmas away from home Caroline was in her element in the kitchen.

"We will have a good traditional, festive lunch", she declared, "but in true Ozzy style. There will be turkey escalopes barbecued in my signature sauce, with roast butternut squash, potato salad and a side of ham for Boxing Day. Dearest, what would you really like for New Year's Eve?"

"Battered cod, oven chips and mushy peas", Jones didn't hesitate. He was making a joke but Caroline took him quite seriously.

"I can buy Atlantic farmed cod, make my own beer batter then brew up a vat of marrow fat peas that just need a good boil and mashing. Not my usual meal but very quintessentially English. Right Cedric, we won't forget to sing Auld Lang Syne at midnight while the Corporation will be putting on a big display of fireworks over the harbour bridge. We celebrate several hours ahead of Old Blighty but after New Zealand. What fun!"

JUDGE JONES RESURGAM

II. Meanwhile Back at the Ranch

Episode 1 - Court House Blues

Michael Charles relaxed at home with Holly, his lady lawyer wife and their young baby son, now christened Paul Edward Charles.

"I had an email from Jones as he comes to terms with retirement and his new life of luxury and ease." Michael smiled, cradling young Paul in his arms as the proud father held a cooling, teething ring.

"I have had a light bulb moment", replied Holly, "it wouldn't do anyone any good if Jones suddenly up sticks again and comes back, it's a huge trauma to do once never mind twice. But remember from your barrister training that hierarchy of need from Maslow, studied over many decades. Jones has every luxury that money can buy but he needs fulfilment and a new dream to cling to".

"Yes that's so much a great truism", said Michael, "he mentioned in his email that he is hugely enjoying new hobbies of pony trekking on the beach plus he's taken to exhibiting his own water colours in the church rooms but he hankers after Court House life".

"Shall we speak to him using the computer again? That way we may be able to encourage him in all he is achieving. We don't really want him returning to City as it could interfere with your progression in your own career". Holly took baby Paul and laid him on his back for sleep then Michael switched on the consol.

Jones was really delighted to speak with them both, he said everything that was flattering and appropriate about their first child then called his second wife Caroline to join the conference.

"Michael, I do have a new dream that I've held for a long time even though I'm not a Member of any Parliament and can only act as an adviser using my legal knowledge and experience. I would like to assist in the reform of the Mental Health Act as I followed its progress when I was first training for the bar."

"Jones I know that mental health is the Cinderella of the health service and my own MP has advised that it's difficult to gain enough parliamentary time. There has been a lot of talk recently about how the Police shouldn't be involved as they don't have the required specialist training or expertise. It's even made the headlines that people who have committed no offence have been held in police stations while they find a bed in hospital for them. You would certainly be doing a very valuable review and it's most definitely something to get your teeth into. Keep us informed, you can access the reference library online and I will consult with psychiatric staff in England. You can always visit and maybe see your grandson who is growing up fast."

After the conference, once his computer was switched off, Michael prepared to leave for the City Courthouse.

"Nulla in mundo pax sincera", quoted Holly, "there is no peace in the world. It's just playing on the radio". Michael laughed and headed out to work.

At the busy court, Michael was defending a new case of an eighteen year old man from a steady, secure home life who had parents of good standing in the community. Michael quickly observed that his latest client had poor diction as the astute lawyer couldn't always make out the story presented to him. The young adult had been arrested for affray and a serious charge of grievous bodily harm. The young man vigorously asserted that he had no knife, had been just having a quiet drink, but then became inarticulate as questions continued.

The statement from the Community Support Police Officer who had made the arrest at The Scallop Shell Tavern, Shining Sands, had this much to say.

"The young man is named Jon James. An ordinary youth doing fairly well at school but caught up in a fight at this popular, seaside hostelry where a knife had been seized. There was a stabbing but fortunately the victim has been discharged from hospital and is recovering at home with a wound to his upper arm. It seems that the victim had put up his arm to protect his face and also his younger sibling, also eighteen. Jon James had been caught on camera arguing, pushing and shoving then holding the knife. His teachers were shocked and appalled, saying that he'd not been in any kind of trouble before. They said that his diction was often poor despite many referrals to speech therapy".

"Thank you Nigel", responded Michael, then he asked to see his client again to advise an early guilty plea. But he said to Mr. James, that his defence was poor and asked "Were you provoked?"

The defendant nodded and then the attendant court official offered pen and paper before taking Jon back to his cell.

"It's going to be a long day", the attendant remarked to Michael who merely asked to hear the dictaphone recording of the police interview then suggested to His Honour that a speech therapist be called.

Episode 2 - A Revolving Door

Michael was in his office the next morning when a tap on the door proved to be a visit from His Honour Judge Mildew.

"Michael", the Judge began in his measured way, "Pemberton has only come back from retirement until we can recruit a new replacement but in the meantime I have been looking over the case notes for Kylie Smythe. She had an adjudication and was sentenced to an extra fourteen days for an affray inside jail but I'm hearing that it's happened again. She is in receipt of certain monies from relatives which all goes into a savings pot but she is still in contact with people who paid her for weapons. You are my best expert Michael, can I prevent her friends and family from feeding her life of crime?"

"The Law is an ass", quoted the wily barrister, "but it's still the Law. I know that she would have to pay back the proceeds of crime through the courts. The relatives could argue that the money they pay her is for her vaping, treats and phone credit but my first question must be, as with any business, who bought those weapons from her because those said relatives are my first and last suspects".

Holly Charles nee Herbert was preparing for her return to busy court life after her maternity leave. Michael wanted every proper care taken of their son, so he took time to help Holly interview the new nanny. A young lady was engaged, started straight away and proved to be efficient, capable and kind. The loving couple were pleased as well as relieved as Holly began to explain to the new nanny where to find all Paul's baby things and where to dry everything.

"It's a wrench", she admitted, "but I don't want to lose all my legal skills. Plus I want to have something to discuss over breakfast besides nappy talk".

"It's so good to see you back Holly", smiled His Honour Judge Mildew, "it's nice to have a familiar face when there are so many new recruits getting younger every year". Then she set to work listening to Jon James with the help of an expert speech therapist.

"You are advised to plead guilty", she was firm but fair. "There is evidence from the CCTV footage, eye witness statements plus a statement from the arresting officer".

Jon James arrived at Shooters Hill jail to wait for his next court appearance for sentencing.

"Remand is the worst time", other offenders spoke from their own experience, "it's the not knowing. Once you know then you can see an end point and plan your time". Probation appeared from nowhere after a few days and asked Jon how was he spending his time inside?

"Scrabble with my mates", he said quite distinctly.

"Don't see prison as a revolving door", advised the supervisory officer, "use time to take advantage of what's on offer. You have good English and Maths, you need to focus on the positives. There's distance learning if you couldn't get to Uni, after your course you could become a classroom assistant while you're here".

"S.O. Modem is being a bit crafty here", said Holly to Mildew after receiving Mr James first letter, "he obviously thinks that an orderly role will force Jon to practise his vocal skills but it's a mystery where it comes from".

"Psychoanalysis is not my first calling", insisted Judge Mildew, "I would see it as behavioural especially as it seems to come and go as if at will".

"It doesn't excuse the gravity of the charge, most assuredly", agreed Holly, "but it's worse under pressure and if he needs a meal. When I next have my meeting with my husband I'll ask if he got any sense out of the therapist".

Probation met once more with Kylie, finding the offender in her cell concentrating hard on some knitting project. Kylie was asked if she was getting bored and would she like to attempt her English and Maths assessment?

"I tried it in school", Kylie suddenly remembered, "but I didn't understand half the questions. You explain the difference between a fact and an opinion".

"An apple is green, that's a fact, but chocolate is nicer, that's an opinion", replied the officer after glancing around the rather disordered room. Kylie smiled in spite of herself then admitted the time was dragging.

"I will have to do something, give it a try perhaps. I'd like to do art." Then the probation officer encouraged Kylie to check the list of courses, apply for her assessment then left her to continue knitting.

Episode 3 - Beneath the Surface

Back in Sydney, Australia, at the huge Central Library, the staff member was exceptionally helpful.

"I think Sir", she suggested to Jones, "that your best bet is to follow updates to the English Mental Health Act online as it's the most advanced version. I can show you how to mark your place with a bookmark but be aware it's a very long document. You will need to allow plenty of time to see it all but if there's a section that interests you most, you can fast forward". Jones said that his particular interest was in guardianship so the librarian found the relevant section then left the former High Court Judge to study the Law with a pen and paper by his side.

"How did you get on?" Asked Caroline later.

"The old order has changed dramatically", he answered, "but the problem is, with every change people get left behind. Also all change by its very nature meets with fierce resistance from some. When the old asylums closed they were replaced with modern psychiatric units and meaningful daytime activity became all the rage. The Day Centre took over as service users quickly became institutionalised in the community. Hostels are gradually being closed as clients are discharged into independent flats, with or without support, but I still hear clients complain of fellow prisoners, for instance, with little or no independent living skills. Here service provision has a vital role to play almost like surrogate parents promoting independence while being a source of advice. The old days of doing everything for service users has no place now".

"Does it need an Act of Law though?" Caroline gave him a challenge.

"It does", argued Cedric, "because service provision is key and has had to modernise, its name has even changed from supported living to independent living. But I'm sorry Caroline, I got carried away. How was your day?"

"I sold a watercolour painting in the church rooms so I feel very good. I've made 250 dollars and treated us to a special, brand name double chocolate ice cream as we rarely indulge. My customers were a younger couple setting up house together."

"That's amazing", cried Cedric, "so we are having a posh pudding".

"I put the remainder of the money in the account we use to buy more special paper and paint", she finished, really pleased at his delight.

"You really are my Agnes", said Cedric, "and this afternoon I spent just an hour counting my blessings as my homesickness vanished".

As the sun set once more lighting up Caroline's villa and private beach, Cedric switched on the local radio station to hear the evening news.

"It's not real is it darling?" Grumbled Jones as the newscaster enthused about a newly released film breaking all records in the box office.

"What they don't tell you is how much it cost to make the film and how much of that money really is profit", answered his wife, "but taking the radio literally always did make me feel inadequate. What's the plan for the weekend Ceddie?"

"Shall we take our paints and easels over to the rock pools further along the shoreline? It's cooler at the moment and dry so we could paint the waves crashing at the point".

JUDGE JONES RESURGAM

III. The Perfect Blank Canvas

Episode 1 - Climbing Mam Tor

Just a week after being released from Tawny Down Prison, Marj, Jones former wife, was shown her new flat close to all the amenities of Buxton Spa town centre. Marj had plans to spend some money she'd saved on the first month's rent, white goods and an easy chair. She was finally able to claim her pension from the work she'd had when younger, in the early years of her marriage. Claire, her daughter, helped her buy a phone to use for an online grocery shop and the little grandson presented her with a family photograph in a frame to hang up in the lounge. Then Claire took Damian home and Marj had time for an autumn walk in the area plus she searched for details of local buses.

Mam Tor is the highest point in the Peak District National Park with access from a footpath at Edale. Marj found details of a bus, planning an expedition with a picnic for her first weekend of freedom in a long time. Birds were singing while wraiths of mist hovered over the stream in the valley of Edale as Marj joined the footpath from the bus.

Mam Tor loomed above her, there were a few other walkers, then a signpost pointing up a flight of shallow steps where the paths and fences had been restored by local volunteers. The wind began to pick up, the mist dissolved and conditions were near perfect for walking.

Marj had spent some of her time inside working on the treadmill of the prison gym, plus she had walked the grounds many times, always looking ahead to a time when she could achieve this lovely walk in the real world. Once she reached the peak the wind was strong but she clung to the concrete post that marks the highest point used by map makers and for navigation. She had a 360 degree view of greenery, fields and peaks and a change went through her mind. She felt remorse, realised that Cedric had been quite indulgent and after playing the blame game for a long time also awoke to the knowledge of how much her daughter was to her and how she had wanted the pregnancy as much as Cedric.

"There is no going back", she mused, "but forwards to cook a meal just for myself, to find a walking group, a luncheon club, a craft fayre then I will teach Damian to play Junior Scrabble".

Damian sat down to a hearty supper after cycling home from school with the cycle bus. He agreed that he would like to play Junior Scrabble as his parents had taught him the alphabet. His nana started with very little words and as they went along she built them into little sentences such as 'the cat sat on the mat'. Then after he'd gone to bed Marj said to her family that she wished them a perfect time if they wanted to visit Claire's Dad.

"We've opened a special savings account and have sent off a photo of Damian", said Claire, "did you enjoy your hike?"

"Oh I really, really did", said her mum, "I have also found a sewing class at the main library. I'm looking at fabric in the department store tomorrow, plus next week also at the library there's a volunteers' morning. It may give me the opportunity to utilise my social work expertise as they're advertising for people to free up parents and carers to give them respite. I need references but to gain experience I can start after finishing at the sewing class which is time limited".

Episode 2 - A Visiting Judge

His Honour Judge Calveston arrived at City Court House with his laptop and a wad of paperwork.

"Man, the traffic's terrible", he exclaimed to Michael behind the scenes. "I'm here to help Ms Smythe as she is not settling in very well at Fallow Fields. She's had two adjudications for affray inside".

"She is finally doing an art course which is some progress", answered Michael.

"I'm called in to ask her to come clean about where she buys her weapons and to whom are they supplied? New legislation now means that she can be sentenced to more time for a failure to cooperate but also if she complies she can receive a positive comment and be eligible for early release with supervision. She was only given a year but new evidence has arisen of an ugly trade in cross bows that are nasty, offensive weapons. You spoke with her?" Calveston had made good progress.

"A tactic used by probation was to question her client Mr Skinner", said Michael, "but there are others, some of them in the devolved nations. With her arrest and a threat being removed, insiders are starting to open up. It's early days but have you met Skinner?"

"I'm vexed, in fact I'm bexed that it's taking so long", came the reply.

Michael was pleased that the visiting judge was taking such a concerted interest in this difficult case so the experienced lawyer put in extra time to fill out all the paperwork needed to get Calveston to meet with Harry Skinner. The convicted felon, previously known as Slashing Harry, was now anxious to come clean and improve his image by complying in full with this cross examination. Harry was soon to be released after a positive parole hearing but his future lay in the lap of the gods he felt as Kylie had disobeyed probation and tried to contact him. His Honour Judge Calveston was finally given the required clearance to visit Harry at Shooter's Hill Prison and it was going partly in the judge's favour but there were areas of Kylie's dark life completely unknown to Harry.

"No, there was no relationship but she supplied knives when I was banned from using the Internet. I haven't had any crossbows or guns, no I never", asserted Harry.

Calveston went on to question Harry about Kylie's other customers then the senior judge reported back to Michael Charles that he was well pleased with the interview. "I'm feeding this information back to Detective Chief Inspector

Frankley and there should be more arrests on the way", was all the judge would say.

Episode 3 - Old School Communication

Mail was delivered to a tin box outside the front of Caroline's villa and when she went to check one afternoon, there was a letter for Cedric.

"This came for you", she announced as she handed him the envelope.

"The handwriting is my daughter's", said Cedric, a bit startled. "Claire has kindly let me know that her mother has been released from prison, with a new flat in the Peaks and she has everything she needs. She just asked that they send the photo of our grandson who will be starting at his local school soon, and that's it".

"Would you like to see him?" Asked Caroline.

"It's been a while since we came home from the world cruise, but it's a long haul flight and I really don't want to see my ex wife", was Cedric's considered reply. "Perhaps if we all saved for a year they could come here. I loved my daughter dearly and have a huge respect for her partner. He is a Community Psychiatric Nurse who stays positive under repeated changes, stress and duress, and it's always a tonic to be with him. But Caroline, going back to your phone call when you first invited me over, you suggested we could have our own child. The ties of love are binding, we're getting on so well and you have a wealth of skill to pass on".

Caroline was in complete agreement then Cedric invited his daughter by his first marriage, his son-in-law and grandson to stay at the beach side villa during the Christmas holidays. In his letter Cedric offered a visit to the National Park to see kangaroos and koala bears with a very tempting offer to let Damian ride a very little Shetland pony as Miles had just one or two of this smaller breed. The proud grandfather also sent his daughter an email to thank her for her letter and say that his was just about to be posted.

"I think this Christmas is forecast to be a hot one", said Caroline after checking the news and weather, "so we can also do something like a boat trip across the harbour as there'll be a cool breeze from the water. How are our finances looking now Cedric? If I fall pregnant we'll need to splash some cash on doing up the guest bedroom into a nursery".

"I allowed for all of that", her husband reassured her, "the wedding and cruise are all paid off and the cost of groceries is not rising so sharply. Oils and canvas are expensive but we still have good stocks of paper and watercolour paints. My catalogue the group made has also sold quite a few copies so it's looking really positive".

"Another quintessentially British treat for lunch then", Caroline said by way of surprise, "Coronation Chicken Salad with a few sultanas".

JUDGE JONES RESURGAM

IV. Peer of the Realm

Episode 1 - A Hearing for Jones

"What I'm looking at", said Jones to his son-in-law at a computer conference, "is the detention of service users under the Mental Health Act and the use of major tranquillisers whether appropriate or not. I know doctors can get an undeserved bad press but these knockout drops and sleeping tablets are addictive; we hear that patients refuse their medication for thinking the doctor is trying to poison them which is one reason for poor compliance. For good recovery we need good compliance, therefore kinder treatments.

Patients no longer want to sleep until two o'clock in the afternoon then be up all night. Modern service users want work, activity and to lead full, rich lives. It does seem inhumane to detain a client for three whole days just while the doctor makes a decision. All of that when the client has the perfect right not to take the beastly stuff. The Law is an ass".

"It's been the status quo for a very long time and those tranquillisers are only prescribed for short term therapy", argued Samuel, "also there are advocates who can see the patient when they are compos mentis enough to understand the proceedings".

"We're not bound to agree if you have to get well to receive your rights", said Jones who was determined that what seemed so flawless on the Internet, which infuriated him looking back, should realise the overhaul it really deserved. "Not all service users commit crime but are often treated as if they have done so just because they're unwell. They spend many hours in police cells waiting for a decision, let alone a bed. But Samuel you're young and I really respect you even though I believe passionately that the status quo must change".

"What will you do after it goes through the Upper House, or Lords?" Asked Caroline later.

"The next step for me is definitely more reform. I heard rumblings from my former colleagues that every good man or woman passing through the courts calls it the Criminal Injustice System. Just stop to reflect for a minute, the client comes before us for ten minutes and is told how to plead. If they plead guilty they get no trial then they get put on Remand in a jail for up to a year before the judge pronounces sentencing. Every time they see a barrister they get ten minutes of self defence then it's ten years of their life ruined sometimes almost beyond repair. I see a different perspective now with hindsight which is a wonderful thing."

"It sounds like you've been under a lot of pressure", agreed Caroline, "but here's a tip from my experience. Like I sold some paintings this month, you have to sell your reforms to your MP on paper to get heard in Commons then Lords to make the changes you need. You have to keep your patience, persuade politely but firmly, then appeal to his or her sense of justice plus their desire to do good. Put it all on paper, edit it as you type it up, then attach it to an email in addition to posting it. Our great-nephew Miles had to sell his prize steer, it was a beautiful bull calf with an immaculate pedigree worth hundreds of dollars. Miles made the sale but not without working for it. No Cedric, you've made notes now for some formal representation. A good lady of the local church has the opinion that modern illicit substance misuse starts with an over reliance on prescription medications. We're rooting for you".

Episode 2 - Parliament Opens

The weather was warming up as Caroline exclaimed how nice Cedric looked in his cool, cotton, canvas jeans and open necked linen shirt.

"It's quite smart. Are you going to an art fayre?" She asked.

"I'm driving downtown for a coffee appointment with my Australian opposite number", said Cedric. The Australian High Court Judge was genial, friendly and relaxed in shorts and leather sandals.

"I think it's great what you're planning", he asserted, "but what's your plan for change? You've identified what you disagree with but how will you improve on what you consider to be a broken system?"

"Well", replied Cedric, taking in a deep breath, "we already have alternatives to medication. The family doctor can prescribe walking, gym, horticulture, art, the list goes on, self help books, T'ai Chi. There are innumerable distraction strategies to enhance mood safely".

"It's excellent and I rejoice with you", said a doubtful Australian Judge, "but it's only any good, if people find out. Normally, the family doctor will only prescribe something if the patient asks and knows what they need".

"It needs a nationwide advertising campaign", Jones was ambitious. "People feel let down because they visit their doctor and mostly receive a script. It needs education but let's face it, like with a lawyer, you only get a few minutes in the surgery to get your point across. We know that modern society pops pills, there are big promotions of vitamins and chocolate is a lot cheaper than fruit. But getting back to what we were first discussing, depression can be lifted by fresh air and exercise promoting better sleep. Many of my clients believe in both medication and holistic approaches. What I'm trying to change is the criminalisation of mental health where a community treatment order is too similar to supervision under probation after a custodial sentence."

"It's the temptation to mass all clients under the same umbrella", admitted the Australian Judge.

"Well what I'm really looking at", continued Jones, "is the pulling together of all parties across the health care team. It will need investment of resources of time, money and a better structure to training. Start them young, clients tell me that in hospital they sleep all day then watch television and smoke all night. There is too little to do in the hospital and what there is outside is always time limited".

Cedric came home to Caroline feeling he had acquitted himself well, there was another letter from his daughter Claire and Caroline had organised his spare key for the mailbox. Caroline showed Cedric how to watch an English television program online so that he could tune in to the State Opening of the Westminster Parliament when the time came.

"Fingers crossed, the renewal of the law may get a mention in the King's speech". She was supportive as she sensed he was a little nervous about the reception of his pet project with his MP in England.

Episode 3 - On the Agenda

After almost two months had passed, a letter arrived for Jones from his British MP. It was good news as the City representative was preparing a white paper to upgrade the legal framework for mental health service users who were reluctant to take medication or who were keen to use alternative strategies. The right honourable member for City also made the pithy observation that attempts to make medication compulsory were usually counter productive. However, the letter continued, we have very positive experience of the rollout of immunisation for the pandemic where careful, sensitive advertising was used by local councillors of all political persuasion to encourage lay people to understand that treatment resulted in a much less severe illness. We need to do this in many fields as it's not just psychiatry that reports poor compliance.

"That's a result", agreed Caroline and Cedric. Then the happy former Judge opened his letter from Claire who explained that they had saved hard and could come for the Christmas holidays as the school would be closing early to save energy.

"We can follow the English newspapers from the supermarket or even the library even if they're a bit out of date", Caroline reminded Cedric.

"Yes and eventually the changes will appear on the Act's website once it's been updated. White papers are slow but it's something to look forward to in the New Year when we feel flat after the family has gone back".

JUDGE JONES RESURGAM

V.   What's Next for Jones?

Episode 1 - Staying Challenged

"Revisiting your past for a moment", Caroline began on a hot day when they were enjoying the air conditioning and a jigsaw puzzle, "did you have any qualms about the day of your own arrest?"

"Well, well, that was very stressful", Jones reflected back. "They give you a sheet of paper telling you that you're entitled to eight hours rest but it wasn't born out in reality. I was interviewed from 9pm until midnight then I went asleep until I was woken up at 3am for release as the charges were dropped. I was one of the lucky ones. I had to order a taxi to get home, stop at the cash machine to pay the taxi, then get back to my own car later that day. But one client at least was given strong medication, charged at 3am then woken again at 7am to attend court. No chance of a shower, just two tiny cereal bars and a cup of tea then off you go before the beak in what you stand up in. The lawyer sees the state you're in, advises an early guilty plea and that's the size of it".

Jones paused to wake up to the fact that he had spent his whole former career with this system and only woken up to its flaws once he'd been on the receiving end.

"I have left the old country now", he said, as if to reassure himself, "but maybe there's another white paper due because the clients say that the complaints system is flawed and the volunteers who come in to see fair play, well they're all elderly and have little power. We need decisive action and a deterrent for staff who abuse their positions of power".

Caroline paused on hearing this new side to her husband then fetched pen and paper.

"It sounds horrendous because I know how unwell even I feel after a broken night", she said, "if you have unfinished business with the old country it's not something you can ignore. It's becoming more up to date to uphold the rights of vulnerable people who frequently feel they have no voice. But Cedric you were in a position of very high authority, you have a powerful and persuasive voice with a Member of Parliament back home in England, it's time to have your say".

Cedric made notes on this conversation and would often reflect back on it in later years, he disliked activists and as a student had never felt the smallest inclination to demonstrate or go on rallies, but he was fired up with a sense of injustice now and decided that he would follow up a formal complaints procedure against Custody suite.

Miles 'phoned his great-aunt Caroline to see if they wanted to book pony trekking for the weekend.

"I met Marj, just the once", Caroline gently offloaded after making the booking. "She seemed the archetypal professional wife and mother. Your great uncle has described her as a doormat but she seemed well able to have her way. There is no doubt that Ceddie is completely replenished by his new life but he still needs a lot of support. I'm beginning to understand why one day she just turned and put the knife in but it's the fifth anniversary of my first husband's death so I'm going shopping for a hat for a society wedding we're going to. But Miles, how are you? Have you sold any more stock?"

"We had to say goodbye to our old bull but we have two to replace him. Two fine bullocks that the old man sired out of Daisy and Maisy. Life goes on but dearest great-aunt, perhaps we all need a vacation".

Episode 2 - A First for Jones

Jones kept a journal and he wrote many thoughts on his old life then realised it was nearly time for his first family to visit from England. He and Caroline travelled together to their nearest airport, then in the arrivals hall Claire, Samuel and a very sleepy Damian, gathered around to greet the older folks.

"They say that jet lag is worse travelling East so we came via Los Angeles and will go back via Hong Kong, then it's Westward both ways. Samuel did really well on the flight, he completed his next assignment and emailed it home for printing. But Damian and I played at naming all the clouds and spotting faces in them. We were looking out for Greek gods". Claire said all of this while clinging to her adored father with a hand holding her young son.

"Well my little Adonis", cried the happy Grandpa, "it's chicken nuggets with fries for tea then a good sleep is called for".

It was a hot summer, too hot for walking barefoot on the burning sands of their little beach but on the patio, under the shade of the verandah, Caroline set up a sandpit for Damian to play. She asked the family if they had seen much of Los Angeles and the young couple spoke of driving downtown amongst neon lights and seemingly endless wires.

"After a good night's sleep we can go on the boat trip", Jones said, "we'll see the Harbour Bridge and the Opera House".

Damian, although very young, wanted to see inside the Opera House as he was completely fascinated by the arches and asked his Dad to find out however did they build a house like that with a curve in the roof. It turned out, when they all turned up at the door, that there was a holiday craft session for families with an opportunity to discover all about the history of the building.

Episode 3 - Christmas on the Beach

Caroline was invaluable that Christmas in that she had ordered crepe paper, glitter and safe glue that was everything needed for Damian to make garlands for their lounge plus little cardboard bells to hang on a beautiful piece of driftwood that they used for a Christmas tree. Samuel had brought the driftwood home after searching a little further round the coast where fewer people were scavenging.

"Do you have a metal detector?" Samuel asked Cedric but they didn't really expect to find anything exciting.

"There might be something from as far back as the Penal Colonies but you probably wouldn't find anything older", suggested Miles. "In the Museum there are some coins showing the head of Queen Victoria but I don't think the Romans made it this far from Italy".

In honour of her English guests, Caroline had ordered a goose for Christmas lunch because, she suggested, they needed a bird big enough to feed the whole family. Cedric found an old cookery book in the loft and prepared fresh stuffing using bread crumbs and egg. All in all they had a great festive holiday then once the big day was over, Cedric fulfilled his promise of driving the family to the National Park to see the wild animals. There were displays showing how the mummy kangaroo kept her baby in her pouch and everyone really loved giving Damian his early education.

Miles didn't disappoint, he drove up to the villa with a very small pony for Damian to ride and Cedric walked alongside to avoid mishaps.

"He should remember as he grows up", said Damian's mum and then there was time for some storytelling and a final barbecue before everyone had to go back to the airport for the flight home to England.

JUDGE JONES RESURGAM

VI. Pure Relaxation

Episode 1 - Internal Flights

After Cedric's first family had all flown home to England, Caroline offered a little surprise by way of a summer break.

"It's a hot summer", she said to him, "but up in the Northern Territory there is cloud forest. It's warm and moist, very humid and we'd need to book internal flights in a Biggles plane then maybe have a few days on the North Coast. The signs warn of jellyfish in the ocean but with a wetsuit we could snorkel to see some of the Great Barrier Reef. Make the most of it before we get too old for the insurance."

"I'm up for it", agreed Cedric, falling silent as he contemplated this new plan. "Will Miles come too?" He finally added.

"Yes, with his family. We can stay in a log house which sleeps six. Miles enjoys time on the verandah putting the world to rights. We know that camping is not your favourite so this way we'll have all the comforts of home. We'll go by mule through the forest with a muleteer to lead. It keeps your feet off the ground, away from bites or stings. We'll get you a shady hat with corks although it's a stereotype, life is a world away from the television. Also in the forest the trees are dense so you can't see very far ahead of you, but it's an awesome, surreal experience to ride through the cloud cover. You'll be reminded of Ben Nevis in August".

Jones smiled at this then checked that it would be self catering. Caroline explained that they would stock up on non-perishable food from Darwin.

"A rare English delicacy is planned, that's bully beef hash and Hawaiian pizza which is probably not authentic Italian at all but a taste of Europe and the Americas".

"I will pack our binoculars but I do have a couple of questions", said Cedric, "what's the baggage allowance for a Biggles plane and will there be tree frogs?"

"I will check the details but yes there are frogs, very special ones the size of your fingernail". Caroline was clearly looking forward to sharing this ultimate natural experience. She opened her shopping bag and took from it a selection of glossy brochures from the travel agent at their local shopping mall.

"There's lots to see and do", Caroline advised her husband, "meanwhile we can ask Miles if he remembers going there as a child for an educational trip with his school. He was quite young but always wanted to go again".

At the log house in the forest there was a floor length mirror which Jones could not help gazing in. He combed the fine strands of his thin, greying locks over his gradually balding pate but was very pleased with his own reflection.

"I'm still quite hale", he mused to himself, "with not an ounce of spare tyre, just a well made, chunky look". Then he turned to his wife to observe that all that horse riding must have paid off. Caroline was too preoccupied with reading all the disclaimers for their mule ride.

"It seems, dearest", she responded absentmindedly "that we're not covered for stings or bites or being head-butted by the mules". Cedric followed her into the galley kitchen to read the small print over her shoulder.

"Oh well, it's all booked and the mules are well trained I'm sure", he gave her some reassurance.

Episode 2 - Keeping the Dream Alive

"It's an evening to beat the post holiday blues", announced Caroline as she and Cedric unpacked on returning home to their beach side villa. "A barbeque in the yard just you and me. Miles is great but he talks non stop when he's not tending the sheep and cows, I don't know where he gets it from. Plus I have portentous news, Cedric dear, I'm going to have your baby". Cedric held out his arms then asked Caroline if she wanted to know the sex of the baby from the scan when the time came.

"Yes I will as I'm dying to know", was the eager reply, "I wanted our baby to have a middle name as it's becoming the fashion again so what do you think?"

"Definitely not Cedric but how about George Henry Jones, or for a girl, Rosemary Anne Jones". Jones was looking up names on the Internet.

"Perhaps we could incorporate the name into the decoration of the nursery, as part of the frieze", suggested Caroline.

"Yes we can buy a stencil of bubble letters and just spray over it with gold paint", Cedric really liked this idea. "What did the midwife say about the pony trekking?" He was suddenly thinking that they wouldn't want anything to go wrong.

"My plan is to go to antenatal, gentle sessions in the warm, local swimming pool", Caroline answered, "but if I get heavy it might be too much for the pony if it's hot like last year again. I think I will just have some walks".

Episode 3 - Preserve the Memory

With an ordinary, but state of the art smartphone, Jones had taken some lovely photographs of their time at the cloud forest with Miles and his family. Jones planned to turn this into a lasting memory in the form of a large, wall sized oil painting. It was an ambitious plan and Cedric was nervous especially when the canvas arrived as it was six foot wide. He had invested in this project and was giving it plenty of time although he didn't want to sell the work, he wanted it to be a beautiful frieze to adorn their home.

Caroline was half inclined to suggest painting with emulsion directly onto the wall of the villa but after they'd talked it over she realised that the wall might need repainting and then all that hard work would be lost. Jones drew sketches in his small notebook then practised on much smaller pieces of canvas to attempt to reproduce that sensational effect of sunlight through the cloud cover deep in the forest. Jones was really keen to make this painting work as a huge and wonderful tribute to Caroline for suggesting the beautiful experience of a holiday with a very different slant. Also it was a very potent memory for him as the log cabin was where Caroline conceived their son.

No detail would be missed, the mules were to be included as the experience of pony trekking had been invaluable even though the terrain was very different from the coast. Caroline could see how absorbed and happy her husband was so she left him enjoy his peace while she preoccupied herself with planning for the new baby.

JUDGE JONES RESURGAM

VII.   Enshrined in Law

Episode 1 - A Grumble from Marj

"I'd like to say a word about Fallow Fields jail" Marj announced to her daughter one cold, winter's evening. "I'm all ears", replied Claire, "and I'm taking notes. Can I settle down on your bean bag?"

"They will tell you that you've committed a violent crime", Marj began openly, "but it's a violent environment. Everyday the officer locks up for the evening, slamming the doors and making as much noise as possible then you can't get a headache tablet until the next morning. Every query was answered with 'I don't know' modified by one officer to 'I've no idea'. To get anything done you had to really stand your ground and keep talking. One officer was kind in allowing me to be able to phone my bank for a balance but this really stood out. I was kind in return in helping him find my room neighbour but I wouldn't send my worst enemy there. Tawny Down seemed quieter but just by contrast.

Chapel was loud and proud, many people called us hypocrites, but it was the one thing that made it all bearable. Meditation was lovely, keeping me grounded and it was a relief to get a morning off work. I've seen the officers in riot gear one day then taking part in the concert the next. The music group was fantastic but my ex-husband is right, not all offenders have a mental health issue and not all survivors of mental health commit crime".

Jones read the email from his daughter and laughed out loud.

"I don't know what she expects", he speculated, "despite many officers wanting to help people, it is meant to be a punishment. But we have heard all this before, most officers are quiet at unlocking the doors for evening medication but they are reinforced steel doors. Stay focused Claire is my advice and just one comment for your mother.

Whatever doesn't kill you makes you stronger."

Claire listened to her mother once more.

"Your father did become case hardened and insensitive in his day", said Marj, "but these days a mental health assessment will ask the client if they self harm. If the answer is no then the patient receives no care. Many patients turn to self harm just to get help. But what was the rationale behind putting one client on section 38, in a hospital, with no ground leave?"

Cedric sighed heavily at this comment from his former wife which had all come by email via their daughter.

"One client was kept in a safe space because of all her contacts in the dark world of illicit substances. There had been a death. I would like to bring this diatribe to a close as I have made improvements to the lot of those people who seek recovery rather than dependence on drugs, or institutionalisation. To sum up, my former wife would do well to let go of it all and stick to Junior Scrabble".

Episode 2 - Medication, Medication, Medication

Samuel switched on the computer console for a further conference with his father-in-law and started by thanking both Jones and his wife Caroline for the wonderful time the family had all enjoyed during the previous Christmas holidays.

"Damian was able to draw a kangaroo in his classroom after seeing them at the National Park. The picture has pride of place on the class notice board and Damian has won a gold star. But getting back to the new white paper, it's been accepted by Lords as well as Commons although there were a few dissenting voices, and next time you're in the library you may find it's been accepted into law. Many of the alternative and complementary therapies we hear so much about nowadays have become an accepted norm. What worries me though is that with any treatment, it's still down to personal choice. There will always be many service users who don't take medication and who manage their illness by, for example, making the most of creative highs and sweating out the lows".

"Is it just an old myth, though, that modern illness is really like that?" Jones asked as he was doubtful. "Are there long weeks of depression followed by a super abundance of getting everything done?" Samuel paused then answered in perfect truth.

"Every individual has a unique recovery journey. I really admire what you've achieved Sir, you have played your part in putting an alternative lifestyle on the map. But I still firmly believe in the value of appropriate medication, especially at times of first referral and crisis as clients can be so vulnerable. Here at the community practice where I work, making therapeutic choices is at the heart of what we preach. In practice there's no perfect solution, but we've made some gains. What I don't want to see is medication classed as uncool as it's often essential".

"Just to say in response to that, we've had an agreeable debate but I'm hearing that doctors can be trigger happy with antidepressants as well as sleeping tablets". Jones stood his ground.

"I hear you", replied Samuel, "But our gold standard is to intervene where there's a need and for sleeping tablets, only prescribe them over the short term on a limited basis while encouraging other strategies".

Episode 3 - Pioneering with Persistence

Jones relaxed once all these work related issues were laid to rest, turning his attention to the business in hand of redecorating the guest bedroom in readiness for their new baby. The scan showed a wonderful, healthy boy so they always referred to him by name as George to show how welcome this new addition to their family was going to be. Remembering that Damian had loved the kangaroos and koalas, Cedric planned a frieze of these animals around the alcove where the cot would be sheltered from the morning sun. The mum-to-be reminded her husband of how they had talked of getting a dog so after ruling out anything too big, a puppy was ordered from a new litter on the home farm.

"Now we have a nursery and a gift of baby grows from Miles", said a very pleased Caroline, "everything is set for October, I just hope the male midwife knows his art".

"Speaking of art", reminded Cedric, "it's nearly time for the spring exhibition. I have five paintings and was wondering if you wanted to put some of yours in love?"

Now came a whole new era for Jones and his second wife Caroline, painting was the perfect hobby when the ponies rested and Miles was busy with sowing and planting. Caroline loved free-er watercolour paintings following the Impressionist style but also enjoyed some acrylic work.

"I love the deep, rich, thick and strong colours using acrylics", she said to her tutor, "I find these bolder paints suit my still lives and pictures of bouquets of flowers as there is a greater depth of effect than with watercolour. I love painting with watercolour when I paint sunsets and sunrises as the mood is more subtle".

Cedric was continuing his new kind of landscape from photographs he'd taken during their holiday in the cloud forest.

"It's a challenge to get those mules anatomically correct", he mused as he worked, "with the addition of the muleteer, our family and the luggage. I need to portray the cloud cover, the sunlight through the leaves then the different shades of green and reds of the trees with the bark. This painting will be bigger I feel. I've chosen a sizable canvas, started with the background using a palette knife, then added the finer details with a thin brush. Yes this is starting to take shape and it's pleasing".

VIII. Thinking Art

Episode 1 - An Exhibition Forms a Bond

Caroline packed the cool box full of good things for a picnic as she and Cedric prepared for a trip downtown to see the big city art galleries.

"Here's the plan", announced Caroline, looking blooming in her early pregnancy. "We'll head for the main municipal art gallery to see how it should be done, get some inspiration then have our picnic overlooking the Harbour Bridge as conditions are perfect today".

"No plagiarism mind", warned her husband, half in jest, "I have met many people who tried to copy Ancient Masters but look at a beautiful painting, say by Constable, I never had the skill of painting water like that and think of the attention to detail".

Cedric drove on quiet roads then found parking easy as it was a sleepy Monday morning with half the world on vacation. The main Art Gallery was blissfully cool, all the exhibits were of great interest with a mixture of European influence plus a large room devoted to indigenous Australian art. The couple had a very agreeable day out, then once they were back at their villa, they planned some paintings for their next local exhibition in the church rooms. Caroline decided to try her hand at the batik, something new for them both.

"See Cedric", she explained, "the design is drawn with wax on fabric, then the material is dyed so that it's left white where the wax has been. Once it's been dried in the sunshine, you can scrape off the wax leaving a pretty pattern".

At the exhibition of their art and craft in their local church hall, Jones manned some of the sessions to talk to visitors and hopefully meet with prospective buyers. He also enjoyed talking to fellow artists, finding out where to get the best deals for supplies of art materials. Just imagine Cedric's surprise and delight when he received a visit from his opposite number, the Australian High Court Judge.

"It's good to have a hobby", the younger man approved, "I'm hearing from dispatches, that your new guidelines have been accepted by the British establishment. That was a piece of dedicated hard work, well done".

Jones was then able to introduce his counterpart to Caroline who was gracious in her thanks, then she showed her printed cards for sale.

Episode 2 - Jones' Opposite Number

Jones was just relaxing at home one fine afternoon when his opposite number, the Australian judge, came to call, driving up to their villa in his Jeep.

"Mental Health guidance suggests discussing how you might be feeling with your family before going to see a family doctor", the Australian judge explained as he sipped an ice cold drink on the patio. "The trouble is, you see Jones, many ordinary families would not always be aware of subtle changes until a crisis strikes. Also that guidance assumes everyone is playing happy families which is not always the case. Treatment has traditionally only been available when the patient's mental health has severely impacted on their well being. Every colleague or friend can be wise with hindsight but at first, changes building up to a psychotic episode are not obvious and even very self aware patients may fail to seek help in time.

Modern psychiatry is all about spotting signs early but with family doctors just reaching for a script I think Jones what we need is a good training principle put into practice." The Australian Judge lapsed into speaking silence as he waited for Cedric's response.

"Many clients have said they feel unheard with their government, or should I say the media, refusing to acknowledge the disability. Even professionals who should know better work on the principle 'if I can't see it, I don't believe it'. Many, many times I've seen people come before us with a false front. They say they're fine or talk about physical health issues to avoid stigma. The assumed 'normal' person still thinks it's the patients' fault and I think we have made a start, but there is still a whole mountain range left to climb. Recovery is work, too many have journeyed from the hospital to the day centre to the funeral parlour." Jones sipped sparkling mineral water then spoke to his opposite number once again.

"I know that what you say is much wisdom from the perspective of the client's chair. I was hoping that if my

English Member of Parliament for City can help to secure some funding, then my son-in-law is perfectly placed to organise research into improvement of disease outcomes. When the Mental Health Act was made law in 1983 I was advised that research into these conditions was thin on the ground. Biochemistry studies have led to advances in medication but today's strategies involve everything from self-soothe to meditation. But this last may not help those with a severe depression. Samuel, my son-in-law, is very keen to advocate medication but he has been trained to do that. Certainly, biochemical intervention has a role to play but let's see all this in perspective. Living a life with a mental health disorder is a huge challenge in itself but there are few visible signs unless the observer is clinically trained. Mental Health First Aid is an excellent notion but the courses are expensive and how many survivors can afford them? I want to see true empowerment where people with this difficult and life changing diagnosis really can have control given back to them."

Episode 3 - Thoughts Are Not Facts

Jones heard from his son-in-law just a week later as Samuel was enthused enough to jointly put together a grant proposal with his colleagues, line manager and the community psychiatrist. Samuel put together a very neat appraisal of psychological therapies that were now available from his practice in England and he attached the information as a file with an email for his father-in-law to keep Cedric informed of these exciting developments.

Samuel wrote the whole as a summary, referring Cedric to the website if there was any need of further information. The latest therapy sought to help with impulse behaviour that could often lead to crime or, as it's called, dialectical behaviour was making waves and proving effective as a way of preventing re-offending.

"It's not guaranteed to work", wrote Samuel, "but I hoped this brief overview would interest you as I know how keen you are to find kinder treatments but with effective results".

"He really is as ambitious as anyone could hope for", Cedric spoke to Caroline. "I wonder what Damian will grow into. This is amazingly positive, but some critics would argue that it's a bit like brainwashing. You are meant to eradicate your mind of thought because thoughts are opinions and it's essential to stick to the facts".

"Expressing an opinion on the therapy then", replied his wife, "it sounds like it needs a lot of dedicated commitment to stick to the plan. But if they show success already then we have a strong supporter in Samuel who is really growing and coming up trumps. Did you hear from Michael Charles again?"

"Michael is not breaching any confidentiality in his email. All he said was that the Court House carries on as ever with lots of bread and butter cases." Cedric laughed then switched off the computer, reaching for his phone to take a lovely sunset image of the beach.

JUDGE JONES RESURGAM

IX. New Beginnings, New Life

Episode 1 - Miles is Energised

Miles had been planning a grand tour of Europe for a long time and the whole family had been saving hard, in particular from the most lucrative part of his farming business which was the sale of pedigree livestock. The thriving farm was paying well, even Miles' children had added small change from their pocket money while their mother organised fundraising events, everything from bake sales to theatre on the lawn until one day their dream holiday was becoming a reality.

"We're flying to London Heathrow, for a week in the city, then we'll have a whistle stop tour of England before spending four nights in Paris. From there we travel to the Greek islands for the beach plus some culture in Athens, then we'll be in Holland for tulip season then we'll fly home from there. We'll be back in time for the winter in Australia and in plenty of time for the birth of cousin George in our spring, October time".

Episode 2 - Caroline Speaks

Jones felt that his cup of life was now filled to overflowing as he gingerly drove their car home from the Maternity wing of the local hospital. New baby George had come into the world displaying healthy lungs and, thank goodness, everything needed was present and correct. Caroline was so pleased and filled with emotion after the male midwife made the prediction that it would all be like shelling peas. Not quite in fact, she joked with her husband once they were home, but no pain no gain.

After two days of rest Caroline had bounced back to her old self as she prepared her signature dish of marinated chicken breasts, as Cedric fired up the barbecue. George gave them a few sleepless nights but as soon as they could get unbroken rest Caroline spoke from the heart to her second husband.

"This is the future, my love you have made changes as well as making a difference to me and the nursery is a beautiful thing. You have achieved and my first husband was so very normal but the child just didn't come. Then Tom fell ill and we lost a good man but what a transformation has come over our family. Miles has just phoned to say he's coming to coo over baby George, his second cousin".

"We are so blessed", responded Cedric in the same vein, "as I never had a second child with Marj. Finally the dead past is put to flight, but darling here are the official photos from the hospital and my daughter Claire sends warm congratulations on the birth of her half brother. A tip she sends is to book George a school place straight away".

Episode 3 - Joy Unlimited

Jones then, after a challenging end to his very distinguished career, and an unsolved mystery still hanging over his first marriage to Marj, had found both new life and hope in a completely reinvented turnaround.

Caroline had expressed her total happiness and joy after a very happy first marriage that had sadly proved childless. She and Cedric had found each other again after a separation of more than just geography. Caroline was profoundly glad that she'd left that message on Cedric's answer phone just as they first got together. As they settled baby George in his cot with Mozart gently playing, they realised how amazingly far they'd come.

"To be fair, Caz", said Jones, "all of this is far more important than anything else in the world, even having finally found a voice for many things that were irksome before. No homesickness now, no retrograde step, just forwards to hearing George's first word and seeing him take his first steps".

Then a complete surprise in that the Australian judge called again with a christening gift for their newborn son.